The
Noah Cicero
Bathroom
Reader

ABOUT THE AUTHOR

Noah Cicero grew up in Youngstown, Ohio and later moved to South Korea. He's living in Las Vegas for now. His other books include the novel *Go to work and do your job. Care for your children. Pay your bills. Obey the law. Buy products.* and *The Collected Works of Noah Cicero Vol. I*, which contains the popular cult novel *The Human War*, now a major motion picture.

The Noah Cicero Bathroom Reader

by Noah Cicero

Lazy Fascist Press
Portland, Oregon

Lazy Fascist Press
an imprint of Eraserhead Press
PO Box 10065
Portland, OR 97296

www.lazyfascistpress.com

ISBN: 978-1-62105-158-9

Cover Design by Matthew Revert
www.matthewrevert.com

Printed in the USA.

Table of Contents

Nosferatu

His feet keep walking.

A lonely night.

In a city that does not require a name.

The city has a McDonald's, Walmart, several municipal parks, sewage, city water, garbage men, coffee shops, a college, and even some poets.

The city has obese women who sweat when it is hot outside. It has men who think their haircut is more important than commerce. And it has cats that shit in litter boxes and never know the touch of grass on their paws.

This is where Nosferatu walks.

Nosferatu wears a nice black suit and a bowler hat.

Nosferatu stops his feet.

Stands still.

Looks up at the moon.

The light shines down.

He concentrates on the beams.

He reaches up and grabs a beam.

The beam stays in his hand.

He brings it to his face and opens his hand.

The beam stays there swirling in a circle.

He eats the moon beam and smiles.

Laughs.

A man passes and stares.

Nosferatu looks at him and says, "Have you ever tasted a moon beam?"

The man says, "No, is it anything like tasting pussy?"

"Yes, very much, but without all the talking."

The man laughs and walks away.

Nosferatu looks down at his feet and says, "You must walk now. Do you remember how to walk. We have walked like ducks, like athletes, like gods. How will we walk tonight?" Nosferatu bends over and touches his feet and says, "You must walk tonight. We cannot stand here all night. We have to go somewhere and sit and listen to the air-conditioning and indoor appliances or the sunlight will kill you and me. Are you listening feet, we must walk. One foot in front of the other."

Nosferatu punches his feet and they begin walking.

Nosferatu enters an all-night diner.

He looks around and scans the room.

There is a young couple fighting in the corner about the young man's drinking habits.

There are young black men at a table talking about getting girls at church.

There are old Arab men talking in their native language about their back problems.

There are drunk girls showing each other pictures on their cellphones.

Nosferatu finds Ako.

Ako is dressed in a sweater and blue jeans.

Ako waves him over.

Every night Ako sits in the diner drinking coffee, staring out the window. Some nights he reads a book, most nights he stares and makes sexual innuendos with the young waitresses.

Nosferatu sits down across from Ako.

They never look at each other.

The first twenty minutes pass in silence.

Ako says, "The coffee tastes good tonight."

"Tina always throws out the old shit."

"I was thinking about buying a bicycle from Walmart then riding into a wall as fast as I can. Just to see if I can bend the wheel."

"One time, back in Rome, I walked into a bath house and sucked off twenty men just because I was bored."

"That is funny. I remember when you did that."

Nosferatu says to Ako, "I remember this time I was riding a horse back in Spain in 1232. I was doing jumps and all kinds of crazy shit. And this pretty girl named Marisol. She had long thick black hair and a strong body. She watched me in the field for a while and when I went over to say hi she said, 'You're pretty good at riding that horse.' I replied, 'Thanks.' I like getting compliments."

Ako responds, "Compliments are good."

Nosferatu and Ako sit in silence.

Several hours pass.

A middleaged black woman walks up to the claw machine.

Ako says, "She is a serious claw machine player."

Nosferatu says, "She looks serious."

The woman moves the claw over.

She is sweating with nervousness.

She drops the claw.

She gets nothing.

Ako says, "Damn."

She puts more money in.

She is determined.

She tries for a blue fuzzy bear.

It hits the bear's head, knocks it over to the hole. But it does not fall.

Nosferatu says, "She has it next time."

She puts more money in.

Everyone is watching.

Even the Arabs are watching.

She positions, bringing the claw down to smack the bear into the hole.

The claw comes down and hits the bear.

It falls into the hole.

The bear is set free.

The middleaged woman smiles.

The Arabs look happy.

Nosferatu is walking down the street.

He feels okay.

He stops to look at a garbage can. He realizes the garbage can will never be his friend and cannot help him. So he wanders away.

There is nobody on the street.

Nosferatu hears footsteps creeping behind him. He thinks, "There is a human trying to be stealthy."

Nosferatu turns around quickly.

There stands a medium-sized man holding a wooden spear.

The man says, "I've come for you, Nosferatu. You have been alive for thousands of years, but now you will die."

"This is making me nervous."

"I'm going to kill you. I'm a trained vampire hunter."

"You're ruining my night."

"You need to take this seriously. Soon you will be dead."

"Will you be my friend? I'm lonely."

"No, I won't be your friend. I've sworn to kill your kind."

"You're racist."

"I'm not racist."

"Yes, you are. You are killing vampires for being vampires. That is racism."

"No, it isn't. You're all blood-thirsty monsters who kill people."

"That's racial stereotyping."

"Listen asshole, I'm better than you because I'm human."

"I don't care what you think you are."

"You should."

"I should what?"

"Care what I think."

"Why would I care what you think, you're a fucking racist," says Nosferatu.

"Listen vampire shithead, your days are done."

"My days are awesome."

"What the hell is wrong with you? Take this seriously!"

"No."

Nosferatu pulls out a gun and shoots the man in the belly. The man falls.

The man begins bitching, "You shot me asshole, I was supposed to kill you. That was unfair. You used a gun. You're supposed to use your vampire powers. What the hell is wrong with you?"

Nosferatu looks down at the man and then softly kicks him in the belly where he got shot and says, "Soon, you'll be dead. But your body will remain here on the sidewalk. Someone will come along and find you and call all their friends about the dramatic night they had."

Nosferatu walks away.

Nosferatu enters a beautiful office building.

The building is forty stories high.

It is postmodern and conveys the idea to the common person walking by that those who meet in the building have money.

Nosferatu enters the building.

A guard nods his head and says, "Hello, sir."

Nosferatu looks at him with a sad look. Then puts a twenty dollar bill in his coat pocket.

The guard says, "Thank you, sir."

Nosferatu says nothing.

He gets on the elevator and goes up.

He thinks, standing in the elevator, "This is going to be lame."

Nosferatu walks out of the elevator. He hears voices. Many voices saying different things, but none of the things interest him.

He enters a room.

There's a buffet of rare meats.

Glasses of fine bloods.

The room is full of finely dressed vampires.

A vampire named Leo yells, "All right, now we can get started."

They go into another room with a table set up and seats against the wall.

There is also one seat in the middle of the room.

The top ten vampires sit at the table. Minor vampires that cling to the top vampires and hope one of them dies so they may replace them in being a top vampire sit in the chairs against the wall.

They motion for Nosferatu to sit in the chair in the middle of the room. It is a metal folding chair.

Nosferatu thinks, "Fuck, they are going to kill me."

Everyone sits down.

Nosferatu sits on the metal folding chair and squints at the top vampires.

Leo, who always leads these events, begins to speak to Nosferatu, "Nasir is dead. He killed himself three days ago. He walked out into the sunlight and let it kill him."

Nosferatu squints.

Leo continues, "Nasir was the vampire king. He was the oldest vampire besides you. None of the living vampires are close to you in age. All the ancients have died by vampire hunters or killed themselves. Nasir was a great leader. He was always helping the vampires and made sure we stayed strong. You, on the other hand, don't do anything. That is why we are having this meeting. Usually it would be a ceremony and we would be crowning a new vampire king. But instead we are having a formal meeting because from past evidence it doesn't seem like you want to be vampire king."

Nosferatu looks sad and says, "Why is everyone criticizing me?"

Leo, in an exasperated tone of voice, says, "Because you have done nothing in years. Not since the fall of Rome have you done anything. It is like you've been depressed for 1,500 years."

"I used to wear a uniform."

Everyone has puzzled looks on their faces.

Leo says in a calm voice, "Nasir protected you for years. But Nasir is no longer here to protect you. The myths concerning who you were are boundless. But the history of who you are has strangely disappeared. Our historians believe you might be Osiris, Remus, Aristotle, maybe even not one but several of the Caesars of Rome. Is there any truth to that?"

"I am Nosferatu."

Many people in the crowd stare at the floor after that answer.

Leo continues, "You aren't going to answer? You were once a great man, a man of great power, but now you sit there pathetic."

"I'm right here, you see me. This is what I'm doing. I'm sitting. No power here, no greatness, just a man sitting."

"We want to know, what are the extent of your powers? How strong are you?"

Nosferatu takes off his shoes.

Everyone is watching, waiting for something to happen.

Nosferatu takes off his socks.

Still everyone waits.

Then Nosferatu wiggles his toes and says, "I'm that strong."

Leo says to the crowd, "I told you this was useless. He is nuts. But we have to do this." Leo looks at Nosferatu. "Are you the original vampire, and how did you contract the virus?"

Nosferatu, still shoeless, squints at him and says, "In 493 B.C. I was sitting on the side of a creek in Greece with my bare feet in the cool water. I put my cupped hands down and scooped up some water and drank it. I looked around and had a very pleasant feeling. A sixteen-year-old girl was sitting next to me. Her face was soft and her dark brown hair hung down to her waist. She never stopped giggling. She has been dead for 2,300 years."

Leo, after taking a deep breath, says, "One last question, Nosferatu. Do you want to be the vampire king?"

Nosferatu stands up and says, "I have always been king," and walks out of the room.

In a small motel, Nosferatu sits on a chair next to a table. He smokes cigarettes.

Two women sit on the bed.

One in her early thirties.

She is a pretty but hard-looking woman with stretch marks from having babies. She is naked except for a strap-on. She is smoking.

The other is a young girl of eighteen. She is cute and small. She has dark eyebrows. Nosferatu picked her because she looks like an Arab.

The women keep talking to each other.

About their men, and their other men, and sometimes about gas prices.

Nosferatu says nothing.

The television is on. There is a show on about prisons.

The women just had sex in front of Nosferatu. He didn't join in, or even masturbate.

Nosferatu hands them each a one-hundred dollar bill.

They stop talking.

They are looking at him.

He looks at the wall.

Nosferatu says, "That's for me to talk. I don't want to be

interrupted. I would like to give a short soliloquy."

The older one goes, "Okay, you're the boss."

"I used to be a man. I used to fuck. I used to hold the ass in my hands and pump. I would pump and look down at the ass and feel good. A great feeling would rise up in me. I think that is normal. But I no longer feel that. I can no longer fuck with this penis," Nosferatu points at his crotch, "I can no longer hold an ass with any sincerity with these hands," Nosferatu puts his hands up in the air, "I have been alive for a very long time, don't ask how long. I am able to get anything I want, and I have. But I could never change this body. I have always looked like this. This is my face," Nosferatu points at his face, "These are my arms and legs and belly. My balls have never changed. I used to wear a uniform, I have many outfits. I have made bridges, killed many in different ways, have had different habits that reflected different types of personalities, have stood on top of mountains, pissed next to camels in the desert, I have gone by many names. But I have always had the same body. I may no longer fuck with this body with any interest. Pumping pussies or male anuses with this penis can no longer cause any real excitement to generate a rising feeling of goodness. I think if I had a different body I might be able to fuck again. But I can't. I cannot change bodies. I am condemned to this body. I can pretend I'm a god, a peasant, a drunk, I can even pretend I'm a dog. But I can't change the fact that when others see me, they see this face, they see these arms. You know nothing about me, so I can convince you of anything. I could say I'm a lawyer and you would believe it, you would tell your friends you worked for a lawyer tonight. I could say I'm an accountant, I drive a semitruck and I'm a proud teamster. I could say I am a professional bicycle rider. I could pretend to be perky, a go-getter, or a lonely sad creature, or a determined man of adventure and risk. I could smoke and be a smoker or not smoke and be a nonsmoker. But no matter how I behave you will see my brown hair, the several small moles on my face, my white skin, and green eyes. Thank you, I'm done."

The women look away from Nosferatu and go back to talking.

A few nights later, Nosferatu enters the diner and sits down with Ako.

The Arabs and the middleaged black lady are there.

Nosferatu orders a cup of coffee, a rare steak, and hash browns.

As Nosferatu puts ketchup on his hash browns, Ako says, "Nosferatu, people are talking."

Nosferatu does not stop applying ketchup to his hash browns.

Ako continues, "Leo came in here and asked me a bunch of questions about you."

Nosferatu starts eating his hash browns and says, "These are good hash browns."

Ako says, "Leo wants power and he also wants to know how you got the virus. They think if they can find out than they will be able to make a pill or some shit that will allow them to walk outside during the day. Then he went on about the scientific possibilities of this new age.

"Nosferatu, seriously, can you walk in the sunlight?"

"Have you ever seen me walk around during the day?"

"No, but I'm never out during the day."

"That's true."

"So can you?"

"I can do many things."

"Nos, I'm your friend. You can tell me."

"Once Ako, I was bored. So fucking bored. It was the mid-1800s and I was in America, drinking in a bar. And I thought it was time for another experiment. I like to experiment with humans. They, like us, have many possibilities. I don't mean, like getting a good job, but something more. I looked for a human, a total pathological liar. Most pathological liars don't have confidence, but I was looking for one with confidence, one who could convince. I eventually found one. Oh, he was nuts. He was sad. One of the saddest creatures I've ever met. He was so sad he didn't even know it. He was convinced if he could just make meaning, he would have meaning. Not knowing meaning came from the outside. I made all these little gold plates and wrote ancient letters all over them. And showed them to him saying a great many things. Then I translated the plates telling him a bunch of crazy shit, I mean absolutely crazy shit. Much more insane than there being vampires caused by a virus. And he believed it. Well, I don't think he believed it. But I knew with such a good story told with some confidence to some very sad lonely people, they would tell themselves they believed it also."

"You're saying you're the angel Moroni who visited Joseph Smith?"

"I was really bored."

Ako says, "Nos, you have to listen to me: Leo wants the power. And you don't want it. You should just let him have it."

"They are all short, flaccid penises."

Discouraged, Ako says, "So why don't you allow Leo to lead then?"

"None of them understand the art of being a vampire. We are a people that may live forever and do not get sick. We don't even need to eat. But all they want to do is sit around and be vampires. I found that really lame."

"I fear Leo may try to harm you. He is getting a lot of them against you."

"Then he is leading?"

"Well, I guess."

"I do not want to lead them. If you cannot lead yourself I do not enjoy your company."

Nosferatu finishes his steak, stands up, and says, "Tell them that if trying to kill me gives meaning to their meaningless lives, then so be it."

Nosferatu drives down a dirt road deep in the woods of Pennsylvania. He is going to Alexis's, his old bodyguard.

Nosferatu found Alexis in 272 B.C.

He was traveling through Turkey and heard a story of a twenty-year-old woman whose family was attacked by bandits. The bandits killed her whole family in front of her. She escaped carrying a sword and bow-and-arrow. She lived in the forest for several weeks alone eating nothing but bark off the trees and drinking water from puddles. She found the bandits eating together one night beside a fire, seven total.

She shot five arrows in less than ten seconds and hit five hearts.

There were two left.

They ran into the darkness to face their enemy.

She sliced each of their throats.

She walked into the village covered in blood.

She was not crying and no one has ever seen her cry.

Nosferatu heard of this: he knew if a mere human could inflict such violence, then if she contracted the vampire virus, it would make her even stronger. For the virus gives the vampire twenty times the normal strength and ups their hand-eye coordination tenfold.

Nosferatu found her sitting on a tree stump beside the house where her family lived.

He went beside her, smiled, and bit her politely.

When she awoke a vampire the next day, he told her he was her family now. She said, "Thank you." And she became his bodyguard.

Alexis now lives in a cabin in the backwoods of Pennsylvania. She has lived alone for many years. She is basically illiterate and suffers from emotional problems.

Nosferatu knocks on the trailer door.

The door opens and there stands Alexis.

She hugs Nosferatu and says, "Nos, you need me. You can use me."

"Yes."

She releases her hug and they walk into the cabin.

A fire is lit. Deer antlers hang on the walls, along with a giant moose head.

Nosferatu sits on an old couch.

Alexis starts a pot of coffee because she knows that is what Nosferatu likes.

Alexis says, "I did five-thousand pushups today."

"That is good."

"It took a while, but I eventually finished. I have never stopped training."

"You are a good bodyguard. We used to wear uniforms."

Alexis hands him a cup of coffee and says, "We will wear them again, Nosferatu."

"I hope so."

"Follow me."

Nosferatu follows Alexis outside into the darkness.

Nosferatu says, "It smells wonderful out here, the wind is soft, and I don't hear an unpleasant sound."

She smiles and says, "Come meet my friends."

A minute passes of nothing.

Then several deer come out of the darkness and walk up to her.

She pets the deer and says to them, "You are my friends, aren't you? I like you." She says to Nosferatu, "Look, these are my friends now. I have been alone for a very long time. I made new friends."

"I need you now, Alexis."

"I have not been used since World War 2."

"You must protect me."

She puts her face close to the deer's face and the deer licks her face. Then she licks the deer's face.

Several days later.

Alexis and Nosferatu sit on logs next to a campfire.

A car pulls up in the middle of the night.

Nosferatu says to Alexis, "It's Leo. He has come to annoy me."

"Should I be armed?"

"No."

Leo walks up to the fire.

Looks at both of them.

The fire lights up their faces.

Leo says, "May I sit."

Nosferatu points at a log.

Leo sits down and says, "You can't hide from this, Nosferatu."

"You like this, don't you?"

"Like what?"

"Giving me shit."

"It doesn't matter if I like it or not. I know what must be done. Someone must be the vampire king. And you are not taking the job. But you and only you have the power to give it to someone else."

"You have not mentioned how pretty it is out here."

"This is business."

"Do you ever feel a sensation of holiness in nature, Leo?"

"There is no God. Why would I feel holy?"

"Politicians never do."

"Politicians never what?"

"Have sensations."

"I have sensations."

"Alexis has sensations," Nosferatu says.

Leo looks at Alexis and she goes, "Grrr."

Leo looks away scared.

Leo says, "I'm not here to talk about nature."

"No, you're here to talk about me. Which is a boring conversation."

"Why are you so difficult?"

"Why are you so easy?"

Leo sighs and says, "Are you going to force me to have you killed?"

"I'm not forcing anything. You are."

"You think this is a joke. There are thousands of years of history and tradition behind this. Thousands of years and you are laughing at it. You are disgusting."

"Wait, and there might be a punch line."

Leo stands up and says, "The punch line will be your death," and walks away.

Leo walks back to his car and leaves.

Nosferatu says, "He's lame."

Alexis giggles.

Nosferatu and Alexis enter a boardroom.

It is the Federal Reserve building in Washington D.C.

They are sitting around a table.

Alexis is playing with an Optimus Prime toy.

They sit for ten minutes, waiting.

Ben Bernanke walks in and sits down across the table.

Bernanke smiles and then looks serious. He looks at Alexis and sees she is playing with a toy. He has a funny look on his face.

Alexis says to Bernanke, "Nosferatu showed me the new *Transformers* movie last night. It was awesomely violent."

Bernanke responds, "I saw it. It was pretty good."

Nosferatu says, "This is my bodyguard, Alexis."

Bernanke says, "Should she be hearing this?"

"She doesn't care about anything we have to say."

Bernanke looks befuddled and says, "Okay."

"So what do you want," Nosferatu says.

Bernanke says in a troubled voice, "Things are bad. It

looks like everything is going to collapse. We know you've personally seen collapses before and maybe you know what to do."

"I do know what to do."

"Well, tell us."

"You have to submit to it."

"No, I'm talking about alternative fuels, soil, prices, monetary systems. What are you talking about?"

"Ben, in the beginning when man first started tilling the soil and building little kingdoms. This could been seen in Africa and in the Americas recently: those continents' little civilizations didn't have money. People did things that mattered. Some people farmed this crop, some people farmed another crop, some people would raise this animal, some people would raise another animal, some would make shoes, some would make shirts, etc. There were niches in the economy. You would go and trade your certain crop, animal or textile at a market. The young would become soldiers and protect the people of the kingdom. After they were done being young they would go farm or be cobblers. It made sense. It worked unless there was famine or plague, etc. Then in some areas there was really good soil and maybe an ocean connected to the land to allow them to sail around to collect goods. Populations grew and people started building useless things. The people that required these useless things to be built or useless wars to be fought did not have anything to barter, they were strictly consumers that skimmed off the working population. So they couldn't barter to get their useless things built, but they still had to keep their workers alive so they could keep them doing more work. So they invented money. Which is a symbol of labor. Money comes from the doing of useless things, created by people who do nothing, given to those who did something that was useless.

"What you are most afraid of, what will destroy money,

is that if it collapses, then the useless jobs will disappear. Everyone will suddenly become useful to themselves and to each other. If everyone is actually doing things that are useful, trying to survive together, each person doing their thing to keep each other alive, then uselessness disappears and with it, money. After the Fall of Rome, Europe did not have money. The plagues had reduced everyone to a state of being absolutely useful.

"If a person's primary concern is water and food, then money is useless. Water and food become the money. All you know is money. But if you cannot guarantee that a large sector of your economy will dwell on doing useless jobs then money means nothing."

Bernanke looks at his hands for a few seconds, looks up and says, "But what am I supposed to tell people?"

"Tell them to love it. Tell them to submit to the suffering. Tell them it will give them meaning again."

"I can't tell them that. That still implies I lose power. The point of this meeting is for you to tell me how to retain power, not lose it."

"Ben, you aren't that powerful."

"I am the head of the Federal Reserve."

"Ben, can you go and buy a 1992 Ford Tempo with a shitty muffler and drive it around Washington?"

"No, of course not. I am the head of the Federal Reserve."

"So there is something money cannot buy you."

Bernanke sneers at Nosferatu.

Nosferatu says, "It doesn't seem like you have any power but to be the head of the Federal Reserve. You made more money than there is labor being done and in the context of this society could ever be done. You gave credit to build machines that do the labor of twenty men. But a machine cannot participate in the economy. The problem is, you live in a spaceship."

Bernanke says, "This is useless."

"You got that right."

Nosferatu and Alexis stand up, shake Bernanke's hand. Nosferatu tells Bernanke good luck and they leave.

Back in the city without a name, Nosferatu and Alexis are in Nosferatu's kitchen.

It is a modest kitchen not remodeled since the fifties.

It is a warm spring night and Nosferatu has opened the doors to let in fresh air.

Alexis sits smiling.

Nosferatu walks over to the radio and presses play on the CD player and says, "Now Alexis, you've been in that little cabin for fifty years. And you've missed a lot. But there's only really two things you actually missed, the only two things that came out of the techno age, Elvis and the lemonshake. And now I give you both of them."

While Elvis is singing "Kentucky Rain," Nosferatu gets four lemons out of the refrigerator. Alexis follows him with her eyes. He goes to the table. Cuts the lemons in half.

Nosferatu says, "Rain in my shoes, can you get any sadder than that?"

Alexis shakes her head no.

Nosferatu cuts the lemons in half and squeezes the juice into the glasses. He gets some ice cubes out of the freezer and puts the cubes into the glasses. Then water from the faucet. Then he dumps in a large amount of sugar and says, "You like sugar don't you, Alexis?"

Alexis shakes her head yes.

"I like when he says 'midnight train.' I've seen a midnight train. I've sat on the side of the tracks, when no one was there, and I saw the midnight train pass. I thought about the conductor alone. And I felt like the conductor so lonesome I could cry."

She frowns a little and says, "I know loneliness."

"I know you do, Alexis."

Nosferatu shakes the drinks and says, "But now, Alexis, here is some happiness."

He hands the lemonshake to Alexis.

She looks at it with the half-cut lemon still floating in it, with the puzzled look of an inquisitive child.

"Hold on, Alexis. Let's go on the porch and sit on lawn chairs."

They go outside.

And sit down.

A huge orange moon shines down on them.

Alexis drinks the lemonshake and says, "I like it, I like it."

"I thought you would."

Two hours pass and four lemonshakes.

Nosferatu says, "Do you smell that?"

"Spring," Alexis says.

"Yes, spring. You always know the truth, Alexis."

"I like lemonshakes."

Nosferatu and Alexis smile.

There is another meeting of the vampires.

They sit together in the giant office building, talking.

Leo sits in the middle of the table.

After waiting for a long time.

The door opens.

Everyone stares at the door.

But no one comes through.

Then Nosferatu and Alexis come through the door riding on beautiful white stallions. The hooves smack on the floor making an echo.

They are dressed like ancient Roman equites. They are wearing helmets, body armor, shields attached to their left arms, brandishing Roman short swords in their right hands.

They are both sneering and ready for a fight.

They park their horses in the middle of the room and remain perfectly still.

No one knows what is going on.

Leo says, "Why are you dressed like that?"

"I thought you wanted war."

"I want you to abdicate power."

"Has any man ever abdicated power without struggle?"

"If you have come for war, then fine."

The door opens again and thirty soldier vampires dressed in black modern military uniforms march in, all carrying crossbows with wooden arrows. They encircle Nosferatu and Alexis. Their arrows are pointed directly at their hearts.

Nosferatu and Alexis show no fear.

Their faces remain peaceful.

Leo says, "As you can see, everyone is unified against you."

Nosferatu puts his sword away.

He raises his right hand in the air and snaps his fingers.

Everyone is frozen cold except for Leo.

Leo looks around the room and sees that no one is moving, blinking, it looks like they are frozen in time.

The only other person still able the move is Alexis, who is giggling.

Leo yells, "What have you done? Have you killed them? You madman!"

"Leo, you have passed the test. You have shown you can identify a problem and then unify people to solve it."

"This was all a game?"

"I gave the same test to Nasir and every leader before him. Some have passed, some have failed."

"You aren't crazy, are you?"

"I am Nosferatu."

Leo stares.

Nosferatu says, "I'm going to snap my fingers and abdicate. If you ever need advice, I'll be around. Never tell anyone of this conversation."

Leo nods his head yes. Leo looks sad. He thought he had

power. Becoming vampire king almost seems less worthy knowing the position was given and not taken. But he knows now that he could never take on Nosferatu.

Nosferatu snaps his fingers.

Everyone comes back to life.

No one notices they were ever frozen in time.

Nosferatu says, "I abdicate my leadership to Leo. Listen to him. And if you don't feel like listening to him, then you should kill him."

Nosferatu and Alexis brandish their swords, hold them up in the air, then ride out of the room as Nosferatu yells, "I am Nosferatu!"

A Giant Cat Poem

There is not one song
in my YouTube favorites
sad enough
to endure this night
wearing my khaki work pants
with a small kitty crawling on my lap

The internet is so lonely tonight

The internet is so quiet tonight

It has been quiet for a long time
since your router broke

I miss your emails
A week ago I looked for an old email
with naked pictures you sent me
with a huge smile and tits showing

I read over the old emails
there were big bulging emails
with long Gmail chats

but time passed
and your router broke
and the emails became smaller and smaller

You made me fall in love with cats
I got a cat to replace you and your
bulging emails

We used to moisturize each other
in the darkness of your room
after a night of drinking box wine

we used to talk of class
we used to talk
You told me about John Galliano
and I told you about John Rawls
You told me about Duchamp
and I told you about the history of Rome
and it was nice
pleasant

Half my Facebook pics have you in them
There are YouTube and Vimeo videos with us in them
and we don't have the passwords to get them off the internet

We are in movies together
probably the only movies we will ever be in
and we are in them together

These movies will exist after we die
as long as there are machines that can play them

the Gmail chats will one day be deleted after we get old
and Gmail recognizes that we are no longer using their services

they will cancel our email addresses
or maybe Google will go out of business
and the Gmail chats will be gone
all the emails and Gmail chats deleted

Maybe our Gmail chats will exist
in some government super-server
that collects all the Gmail chats that ever existed

You took me even though I have psoriasis
covered in ugly white dots
you still took me

You still took me even though
I lived on a couch

But bad ideas came
We are smart people
coy, with a sense of sarcasm
Internet savvy
we know who Yeats and Sartre are
but that doesn't mean
we know how to live
it makes sense
our minds would like each other
we are inept at getting
what we want

I found a song to listen to
"Will You Be the One" by Melissa Ferrick
an obscure song
but you were always a lover of obscure songs

You are so obscure

that's why I liked you
you were the most obscure
woman in the room

Took so long
so long
to locate a person like you
a person I needed so much
at exactly the right time

Damn it woman you saved me

But now when you need saving
I am helpless

An epic fail
I am just not smart enough to solve these problems
I am too taken by moods

Moods

So many moods

I click Gmail on Google
hoping that when the page loads
your name is there

your name is not there
with a little green dot next to it
it used to be there
but it is no longer there
your router is broken

KOREA
STORIES

How Paranoid Can I Make Myself Tonight

Nickelback, on the radio, want to be funny, need to be funny right now, need attention, in the car alone, alone driving to Kent, where I met my girlfriend. We met on a Saturday, came in, she was high on coke, she looked beautiful, fell in love, went up to her room that night, had sex, she pulled down her pants, I saw her vagina for the first time, never forget, the same vagina, have loved the same vagina for two years. What is her name? My girlfriend, her name is Maddie, that is her name, I have given her the name Maddie, now she has the name Maddie, oh god Maddie.

Maddie will be there, what time I don't know, she will arrive when it is time to arrive, she will text, she will use her phone to connect to my phone, I'll get her text and I'll find her. I can't find her in that same apartment, she has moved since then. She moved from Kent, I don't go to Kent anymore, other people have moved from Kent, some remain. Kent is a college town, a town that has college kids, professors and Starbucks and college bars, all of them supporters of college.

Really excited now, so pumped, have a Saturday off from the restaurant, I still work at a restaurant, thirty-one years old, total failure, my brother had three kids and a mortgage by the time he was my age, everyone is normal by my age, not me, also substitute for a local school, boring most days, most days, I sit there, checking my email over and over again, the schools have blocks on every website besides Google and Wikipedia.

A Nickelback song comes on, I get my cellphone and record myself rocking out to Nickelback while driving, texting while driving, I am a dangerous person, a person who lives a life of danger and excitement, texting while driving, making movies while driving, I send the movie to Alex and Tom, they both hate Nickelback, maybe it will entertain them, play the movie back, can't understand what the music is, complete noise, oh god, my funny joke isn't funny, all I want to do is be funny, why won't the world let me be funny, I'm not funny, I'm not a funny person, I should settle on being a nerd, a nerdy asshole that writes long Pynchon-like novels, I should delete my Facebook and Twitter accounts, go to the mountains and write Pynchon-like novels, keep thinking 'Pynchon-like novels, Pynchon-like novels, Pynchon-like novels, Pynchon-like novels, Pynchon-like novels,' I have never read Pynchon. (I also consider writing Derrida-like philosophy books.)

Get to Kent, text Alex while driving, he texts back, "smoking two blunts, be at Starbucks in a half hour." I don't know what to do, Tom told me he would be at Starbucks in an hour, I left my house, I am on time, I have a cellphone, I always know what time it is.

Go to the Chinese buffet alone. You see me at the Chinese buffet alone. You see me walk among the Chinese food, you see me look at General Tso's chicken, there it is, chicken made all weird, you see me get some. You see me stand near the chicken on the stick things, is it really chicken, who cares, get like five of them, the fried dumplings look good, oh, fried dumplings you supply meaning to my life, will never give up on fried dumplings. Sit and eat alone. Everyone else is eating with someone, everyone else has a friend, someone is eating with their mom, their mom loves them, they don't talk, no one is talking, college kids are sitting in groups of four, they are having a great time, I used to sit with three college kids at the Chinese buffet in Kent, but no more, two of them went to Chicago, they needed to go to grad school, they needed to make money and profit in this world, I need to sit alone at the Chinese buffet, slowly put fried dumplings in my mouth.

I drink water at the Chinese buffet, the water tastes just like water, can you see me eating alone, there by myself, with the Chinese food and water, I am not using a straw, you wonder, "why isn't he using a straw, he is drinking from the glass, that is so gross, he is a gross person that does gross things," these are your thoughts, your main thought is "doesn't he have any friends," that thought goes deep into you, makes your heart rattle around in your chest, your lower intestines contract and cause diarrhea thinking "doesn't he have any friends?"

Go to Starbucks, the line is long, full of professors and college kids, I want to have fun tonight, I want tonight to mean something, I want tonight to be perfect and wonderful like the old days in Kent, when we would take Adderall and drink all night watching the cats play, life would pass easily, feeling overly sentimental, bad, must stop this, put a halt to sentimental thoughts, who asked time to pass, I didn't mean to graduate college, it was an accident, maybe I can go to grad school, but grad school is serious, you have to take a GRE, get accepted to a program and grad school is way too fucking serious to be drunk all the time, oh fuck.

Go to the bathroom and poop, Alex sends me a text message,

says he will be there in twenty minutes, the bathroom in Starbucks has the best lighting, I stay in there a long time because of the lighting, go upstairs to sit at a table and read Mark Twain's *The Innocents Abroad*, reading a classic travel book, getting ready to travel to South Korea to teach English, haven't been hired yet but Maddie has, my girlfriend, I keep telling myself I have a girlfriend, only see her once a week, sometimes twice, not a very active relationship, Mark Twain thinks France is beautiful, I am in a Starbucks in Ohio, tell myself more things, the amount of shit I tell myself reaches scientific notation levels.

Alex shows up, he comes upstairs, drinking coffee, he has Brandon with him, both are stoned, glassy-eyed, faces droop, smiles protrude, Alex says last semester did not go well, Brandon says last semester did not go well, he is washing cars now, Brandon rarely ever talks, conversation about comments on Alex's vlog occur, "Is this all people have to be mad at about, a vlog, an interview, is it worth it, to scream at a person, to personally attack a fellow human for making a vlog, America badly needs a new rail system, Monsanto is feeding us garbage, we have a huge national debt problem, hey but you know what Alex Soso yeah this kid, this kid needs to have his feelings crushed, destroyed, this kid needs to know that he is a horrible person who should never create a vlog again."

Alex and Brandon both laugh, I don't know what to do, I just said something funny, but they are high, is a high audience still a good audience, am I still funny if I make high people laugh, am I just an actor, do I have a personality anymore or have I taken on a persona only to entertain people, am I a real person, do I deserve to have friends, I doubt they even really like me, maybe they do, they came to see me, but late, people who show up late don't really like you, I need to start drinking soon and find some Adderall, if I can just find some Adderall I will be able to write Pynchon-like novels and have normal conversations while thinking about seeming intelligent or being funny.

"Alex, you have any Adderall?"

"No, only pot, have lots of pot."

Is pot a good word to use or is marijuana or reefer better, can't decide, feel discomfort concerning talking about marijuana.

Call Maddie on the phone:

Maddie: I am at Jerry's house.

Me: Can we come over?

Maddie: Oh, I don't know, they are having a serious dinner party.

Me: What do you mean serious?

Maddie: Everyone is eating, I am sitting on a couch.

Me: So we shouldn't come over.

Maddie: I don't know.

Me: Hmm.

Maddie: I didn't know I was in charge of making plans tonight.

Me: You are.

Maddie: No one told me, I haven't seen Rachel and Dee in a while.

Me: I know, you can talk for a while, we'll call Rose.

Maddie: Okay, I'll try and meet you there.

"Alex, I don't know what happened, but I got the impression Maddie didn't want us to come over to Jerry's house."

"Huh, I was just there."

"I don't know, she said there is a serious dinner party."

"What the fuck is a serious dinner party, they are probably just smoking weed."

Brandon stands in silence, he never talks, just smiles.

Alex calls Maddie, Alex lives in Kent, seems to have more power than me in these things, I have no power, I am just Maddie's thirty-one-year-old boyfriend from out of town, old and slightly creepy with a skin condition, Alex lives here, he sees these people every day, he knows what to do, I lead nothing, I am not a natural born leader, have no leadership skills, I'm a grunt, a private, a low-ranked subdivision of humanity trying to find some Adderall and a place to drink beer.

Alex calls several people, he stands at a distance from me and Brandon, we don't hear what he is saying, get the feeling that there are moves against me, that conferences have been put together and the people at the dinner party have found me to be a prick of some sort, probably because of half-truths and distortions, if I could only reveal the truth of what happened, of what really happened, but no one would believe me, realizing I never believe anything they say, how could they believe what I say?

Do I really like these people?

I do, I have nice feelings when I'm around them, but now there are moves against me, people have made moves against me, the whole world now knows I'm a prick who broke up with Maddie via text message for three weeks in the summer and then wouldn't return her calls, but I didn't know she called me back, because I had just gotten a cellphone for the first time in my whole life and couldn't figure out how to use it and didn't realize she kept calling, my heart broke when I found that out, I thought she didn't call, I thought she didn't love me, which implies that I broke up with her to get her to call me, to scream at me that she loved me, my vanity, my need to be loved is very intense, I want people to like me, I want women to like me, I do so many things that I don't really want to do to get people to like me, I don't know if any of this is true, I have no evidence, just conjecture, Alex comes back, says we are going to Alex's dorm room to figure things out, sounds funny, we get into Brandon's car and go to Alex's dorm room.

Walking through the dorm, Alex says, "This is where I live, I walk by a restaurant on the way to my room, this is my front yard," he points to the space between two elevators, "this is my life, I spend my days in this building."

"Does Linda live here too?"

"Yeah, but she is getting new friends, she is adjusting."

Brandon laughs a little.

We walk down a hall, Alex opens the door to his room, it is a small box, a very small box.

"This is funny," I say.

"This is my room."

"Look, you have a little cute bookshelf."

I look at a copy of Pynchon.

Brandon gets Alex's card so he can go to the bathroom.

"You need a card to piss."

"Yeah," looks like he thinks this is all a huge fucking joke played on him by the gods.

I feel weird being in the little room.

We get more text messages, telling us to go to Rose's.

This is where we are going to meet.

I go to the beer and wine store by myself, buy Woodchuck, there is a bar now in the store, a bunch of frat boys are sitting there, I buy cigarettes, always smoke a lot on Adderall, hopefully somebody will have some at Rose's, getting very intent on Adderall, feel like I'm not having a good time, feel like I should just drive home, there is obviously deception taking place against me, moves against me, things that I don't know are being said about me, I shouldn't have broken up with her via text message, but I get moods, I have moods and they are terrible, all-encompassing moods of fear and anxiety that women do not love me, that no one loves me, that I should destroy everything, there was no evidence that she did not love me, the truth was, she was having a mood too, and then I was having a mood, but my moods are more self-destructive than her moods, I can understand self-destruction, if you can't control things to make them better, you can at least control them to make them worse.

I leave the beer store, in the parking lot alone, you see me, in the parking lot, snow everywhere, freezing, cold weather, wearing a new pea coat I got for Christmas, you think about me being alone, going somewhere with friends to drink beer, you don't know there are moves against me, that there is discussion on how I might not be the best person in the world.

Get in my car, phone rings, it is Tom, yes, Tom.

Tom: Did you see the new bar inside the store?

Me: Yeah, there were a bunch of douches sitting there.

Tom: You should get a taco at Taco y Taco.

Me: What the hell is Taco y Taco?

Tom: Taco y Taco is a place where people get tacos.

Me: Taco y Taco?

Tom: Taco y Taco.

Get to Rose's, have to walk up an old staircase, can't quite remember which door is her apartment, haven't been there in six months, maybe longer, open the door and see an old rotting Christmas tree, hear people say my name, the apartment is old, feels like a trip to the past, walk in the kitchen, the lighting is low, everything seems dark, the room is full of pot smoke, Alex keeps rolling blunts to smoke, everyone keeps rolling blunts, Rose makes me show her my skin condition, she is impressed by the progress I am making, I tell her I am tanning four times a week, a guy I don't know is sitting there, he is dressed like an old Jewish or Italian man who is retired and lives in Florida on a pension, I don't understand it, he is better dressed than me, but I think I am more attractive than him, Alex rolls another blunt, eyes bloodshot, wearing a Cleveland Cavs baseball hat he got for Christmas, Rose sits on the only cushioned seat wearing something comfortable-looking, she looks like a queen, she wants to sleep with the guy dressed like an old man, the guy tells me he plays piano, Rose confesses to being on academic probation, someone puts on a Beatles album, everyone listens to the Beatles, it is 1969, blunts and Beatles.

Linda arrives, Linda is really nice, probably too nice, has ambition, is doing well in college, she is adjusting, she says to me, "I am finding new friends, I'm really excited, I am getting used to the whole college thing."

"That sounds really good."

"Yeah, you want Adderall?"

The moment has come, the time has arrived, beauty, hope,

life will be endearing and charming once I get this pill in my body, she takes the pill out of her purse, the room has bad lighting, dark with a Christmas tree nearby, everyone else in the other room, it isn't a full pill, just a chunk, a small chunk of Adderall, a dream has come true, this pill will make me want to live again, it will put a jump in my step or whatever people say, she drops the chunk in my hand, I drink it down with a glass of water, I wait for it to take charge, "I feel like, I can't really talk to large groups of people without Adderall, I keep thinking awkward stupid thoughts when I'm talking to people, I want to feel normal, I want to feel like one of those people who never thinks, and just have words being flung out of their face, I want to be a face that talks and doesn't care about what it is saying."

"Yeah, I know."

Maddie shows up, she is wearing a giant fur hat that I told her to buy at Target last week, she got the hat because I said I liked it, she is wearing it probably because she knew I was here, she looks nice, she did her makeup, she might actually love me, I can't be sure though, she smiles at me and kisses me on the lips, she wants me to know that she loves me, she is being nice, then her friends from the dinner party come in, why are they here, they have moves against me, the room fills with people who have moves against me, the room is now filled with silent enemies, I don't know who to talk to, I walk around the room lost trying to make conversation.

Rachel sits down wearing a shawl, the shawl covers her thin body, she looks like she has not eaten well in a few months, she has been in Chicago with Dee, Dee looks thin also, they don't look happy, anxious, they are very stoned, another blunt is rolled, the room is full of pot smoke, Rachel can barely move she is so high, she says, "I work at a factory making expensive wallpaper with Cambodians and Mexicans, it is factory work, we work to live in Chicago, but we don't live in Chicago and enjoy Chicago, there aren't enough jobs, the city has reached its peak, we came after the peak, the peak is over, we came late, we want to move to Cleveland."

"I keep myself busy, I have to, if I am not busy then I start to think it's pointless, everything is pointless."

The blunt is passed to her, she hits it.

Maddie says loudly, "I leave for South Korea on February 20th."

Everyone claps, they are happy for her, I am trying to be happy for her, I am trying to get a job but no one wants to hire me in a location near her because I am a man and thirty-one, she will leave without me, she will leave via text message, she will cry for two weeks then meet a nice British man or a big Australian man who will show her the world, and leave me here in Ohio to check blogs and diddle myself in the darkness, at least I have cats now, I don't know if the cats will replace her, but at least I have cats now, Maddie will be gone, she is not proud of me, she thinks I am weak because I cannot get hired, I want my girlfriend to be proud of me, I want her to think I am capable, I want to make money and bring her out for sushi, I can't, I am failing, I am not doing a good job of making her proud of me, she will slowly lose respect for me and find another man in South Korea if I fail.

Rose tells everyone that Norman is playing a show at the Pebble, a local bar in downtown Kent, the Pebble, a small bar, Rose walks around, notifies us that we need to see Norman,

Norman is a townie, he is a nice townie, the world is full of bad townies, Norman is a nice townie, Norman walks through the kitchen, he has a guitar, it is wrapped in an afghan, I am impressed by his afghan, I don't know where to stand, Alex goes to the door to leave, to buy more blunt paper, he screams, "OH MY GOD," Rose sits next to me, we pretend we are startled but really don't care, Alex says that Tom has been standing in front of the door, just looking at the door, imagine Tom fixing his hair, thinking terrible thoughts about everyone and how lonesome it is all going to be, entering that apartment, full of his fellow humans.

Tom walks in, stands in the corner of the room holding tallboys and a pair of men's underwear in a plastic bag, he explains the men's underwear, there is laughter, I go stand by Maddie for a second, touching her fur hat, there are three people by the sink, four people at the table, a few standing by the Christmas tree in the other room. I don't know who to talk to, I WANT TO LOOK NORMAL.

Stand next to Dee, wonder if it is a good decision, probably not, Dee tells me she was fired on New Year's Eve for having a bad attitude, worked at a Mexican restaurant in Chicago, imagine her walking home, down city streets, probably crying, crying a lot, her skinny body crying tears, oh man, tough image, she told me she was crying, she couldn't stop, she went home to cuddle Rachel, Rachel and her slept nervous that night, two anxious people cuddling in the Chicago night, Rose disappears and we can't find her, it is her apartment and she is gone, I want to find out what Rose did in Chicago with two guys I know online, I want the truth, the facts, the gossip, but she is gone, maybe I'll see her at Norman's show at the Pebble.

Alex comes back, smokes more blunts, the blunt smoking is endless, it keeps getting passed around, it keeps passing me by, going to Korea, can't smoke weed, have to function, have to be normal, have to be a man who doesn't smoke blunts.

Someone starts talking about the word Arabic, someone says they to like to pronounce it, "*a rab ic* and not *ara bic*," for some reason I get the idea this conversation should include me, there is no reason for this conversation to not include me, I've read several books on Arab and Persian culture and want to tell everyone about Arabs, someone from the party is half Egyptian, I ask her if she is a Berber, she assumes I am insane, everyone assumes I am insane, why would I ask someone if they were a Berber, why would anyone ask another person at a party in Ohio if they were a Berber, she doesn't know if she is a Berber, she doesn't care, she responds "Egyptians call themselves Arabic," I am just trying to sound smart, this is what I want, to feel loved for being smart because I am not athletic or actually good at anything, my current real life status is low self-esteem because I can't find a job in South Korea, my current real life status is to prove that I am smart about the peoples of Arab lands, why why?

Why why why?

I can feel that Maddie is like why, why does he do this, does he need to do this, did I really pick this asshole to be my boyfriend, everyone leaves they go other places, Maddie, the Berber, and I walk down the street, snow is scattered everywhere, I look at the flour mill tower above us, try to listen for the river flowing, don't hear the river, it is cold and our cheeks feel a nice chill, a nice soft chill, cheering me up, maybe the Adderall is working, get to the Pebble, not a big crowd, a band is playing, we get drinks and find seats, thank god I have a seat, Maddie sits next to me and says, "You need to learn to take it easy," why is she telling me this?

"You either feel really convinced something will be great or that something will be shit, you can't live like that, focus on Korea, take it easy, you will go to Korea, imagine it, being in another country doing an easy fun job, going to Seoul on the weekends, partying, hiking up the mountains, visiting ancient Buddhist temples, that's life, life is beyond the internet, beyond just writing, write later, I love you, you know, just take it easy, focus on living."

Oh fuck what is this, this is attack, character assassination, I am good at being stressed out good at having anxiety this is my mode this is how I live in stress and fear telling myself things are going to be either really great or really bad does she even love me, should I believe her, my mother used to make conjecture about my existence and none of it was true why would anything she said be true?

Maddie goes to the bathroom, Linda comes and sits next to me, she says, "This bar is kind of shitty," I don't know what to say to her, can't stop thinking about Maddie's verdict on my Being, case closed this man is an asswipe.

"Where is Rose?"

"Don't know, she never showed up."

Rose is somewhere having sex, Alex went back to his small dorm room, he goes to sleep on a thousand blunts, a thousand blunts rolling around in his head, dancing zzz.

Maddie returns, Linda exits.

Norman goes up on the stage, he screams, "ROCK AND ROLL."

I find it nice.

Maddie reminds me this is art for art's sake.

Maddie says, "Let's disappear, let's go back to Jerry's house and go to sleep, we might have to sleep on the couch, we will have to cuddle hard."

Does she still love me?

I put on my stocking cap to face the outside world, we walk down the street, snow cold ice all of the above, stand in front of Rose's apartment door, you see us, you are across the street, you are walking home from the bar too, you are somewhat drunk yourself, you see us, you see a woman grab a man and yell at him, "You are a libra, a motherfucking libra, Jerry and Dee are both libras they are both awesome, they are positive, you can be positive, you can live, you don't have to waste away in negativity, all you have to do is make a choice to do something besides sit around and think negative thoughts, you are a libra," she shakes him, she keeps shaking him, the man looks down at her with a sad facial expression, "People are saying you are bringing me down," she doesn't say if she is fighting them on that accusation, "People think you won't go to Korea, you are going to back down, you are a libra, the scales balance the scales even the weights make an even scale," no one is sticking up for me the guns are loaded the firing squad ready boom.

Maddie walks down the street, the feeling I have is of a person who just got off work, went to Taco Bell, ordered through the drive-thru, drove all the way home, looked in the bag to discover that they forget his chili cheese burrito—yeah a pretty bad feeling.

Walked up the dark steps, walked into Rose's apartment to get my bookbag, the old dry Christmas tree is there, I wonder if it is a metaphor, hear sex noises from the other room, sex noises, the noises of two humans politely fucking each other out of wedlock, Maddie has to go ahead and ask Jerry if I can spend the night, I know what the score is, I know that I am in trouble there are moves against me, walk into the rented house, Maddie leads me upstairs, we go into the empty bedroom that is used for smoking cigarettes, window left open I close it, Maddie tells me she woke up early to go to a funeral, she says the mayor was there, it was an important funeral, I want an important funeral when I die, a long procession.

Go to the bathroom, read *National Geographic*, turn off the lights in the hall, go to the bedroom, Maddie lies on her side, she is asleep, I lie down next to her, don't cuddle her, usually I would cuddle her, but I can't I am mad at her, I feel anger at her for judging me, I don't want to be judged can girlfriends judge boyfriends she is trying to fix me she wants me to be a better person what an asshole, is she trying to destroy me? Why can't I spend my life in a beautiful state of depression, depression is wonderful, a nice place where a human can sit and not be bothered where I can think all the time about shit that doesn't matter to me or anyone else, I want to worry I want my worries to infect my spinal cord and make my back hurt I want to give myself headaches with worrying and self-induced stress please let me be stressed maybe she is right, can she be right should I just act normal she is over there, sleeping (pause, look at her sleeping body) her small sleeping body I love that body I love that woman she is so fun so nice to me but she wants me to be a better person a person who doesn't waste his time and waste away and in general waste but if we live in Korea we will live an hour apart we live an hour apart now why all these hours apart, she thinks she isn't negative how am I negative I have two jobs I spend hours writing a day I make vlogs and drink coffee at Starbucks with friends I am trying to get hired in Korea those are positive things I do positive things and say negative things because the negative things make me happy to say doesn't anyone understand me, I am such a teenager of the 90s (Cobain and Tupac), I look at her she is fine, she is sleeping, she must be fine *with our version of love* she must be convinced of our love she must have faith in it, she is the only one who judges and pushes and crushes and slams my head against things until I do better, need to stay by her side, play with her hair, she rolls over and puts her arm around me, pulls tight, she cuddles me in her sleep her little body her little arm next to me, stop screaming inside your head, you see a man lying next to a woman, her small arm around him.

UPDATE: Three days later the lead character woke to an email saying he was hired in South Korea, and there was no reason to be worried.

THE LOST
DOG

At night, when Justin was alone in his room in the Hanshin Plaza, he would put on a pair of Crocs and take the elevator downstairs. He would walk by the security guard sitting in his little office full of surveillance screens. The security guard would watch television and once an hour take a walk around the building, and every two hours he would go outside and smoke a cigarette.

The security guard never smiled at Justin, who was from America. The security guard didn't care. He thought all American men came to Korea only to take their beautiful Korean women. When Justin walked outside he immediately saw many neon lights advertising pool halls, gyms, hagwons, banks, clothing stores, norea bangs, Korean chicken barbecues, Korean pork barbecues, Korean duck barbecues, and cellphone stores. Taxis, small gray vans carrying hookers, red little scooters (some delivering food), green buses, red buses, and blue buses drove by, each with places to go.

Justin walked into a CU convenience store and said, "Annyeongsayo."

The man behind the register said, "Annyeongsayo."

The man behind the register was in his late thirties. He had strange bumps on his right arm. They protruded from his skin, like a small snake was under his skin. Justin always looked at them. The man behind the register did nothing to hide them. He wasn't proud of them. He just didn't hide them. Justin had psoriasis. Justin enjoyed seeing other people with skin problems. He felt like they were his brothers and sisters.

The man behind the register worked the night shift. Justin was a school teacher at a hagwon down the street.

Justin made a lot more money than the man behind the register.

Before Justin went to Korea, he worked at a restaurant making barely any money, like the man behind the register.

Justin looked at the snacks: dried squid, peanuts, ramyeon, and beef jerky. He bought beef jerky (little taste of home), soju, and a can of Coke Zero. The man behind the register smiled, laughed, because the foreign man was drinking soju.

Justin took his purchases outside. It was summer. He sat down at a plastic table with plastic seats outside CU. He mixed his soju and Coke Zero and ripped open the bag of beef jerky, then he looked at the taxis passing, he couldn't see any stars or the moon. He knew he had to walk about a mile down the road to see the moon and then look at a specific spot between two buildings to see it.

A drunk man walked by. He stumbled, then leaned against the wall of a bank, then slowly slid down till he was sitting on the sidewalk. He closed his eyes and went to sleep.

Justin drank his soju. He remembered America, but his mind didn't go back to the recent. It went back further, to some memory he hadn't visualized in a long time. He was nine years old at the baseball fields (the local Methodist church owned the baseball fields, Justin was from a town of 2,000 people, he was from lonely unremarkable Ohio, he was from a part of America that Koreans didn't care about, Koreans all knew the shows *Sex and the City* and *Gossip Girl*, famous shows, shows that took place in Manhattan, shows featuring the wealthier classes of America, but he was from Ohio, a nowhere place, he grew up in a town where the grocery store had deer and bear heads on the walls, Justin knew how to shoot a gun, he grew up near corn fields, Justin could see the baseball field), but his mind wasn't concerned with the baseball fields; it was concerned with a large log that he would play on by the fields. He liked that log. That log felt safe. He couldn't remember where the log came from. The area around the baseball fields didn't have large trees. There were a few sycamores in the area, but none where he grew up. He wondered where the log came from.

A small white dog came walking by. Justin looked at the small white dog. The cashier came outside to look at the dog. The dog had no owner. The dog was alone, left to walk the streets by itself. Justin threw some beef jerky near the head of the dog. The dog ate the beef jerky. The dog wouldn't get close to Justin or the man with the strange bumps on his right arm. The dog kept its distance. The dog wanted food but it didn't want people.

Justin smiled at the man with the bumps on his right arm. The man smiled at Justin. They couldn't communicate verbally. The man could only speak Korean. Justin could only speak

English. They just smiled and laughed about the funny little white dog.

The dog stayed for a long time, but eventually left. The cashier went back in the store and Justin sat by himself, wondering about the dog. His mind found the baseball fields again. He could see his nine-year-old hands and legs, but not his face. He tried to picture himself in the third person but couldn't do it. He pictured himself in the third person sitting on the street in Seoul, but it made him feel awkward, a scary-looking white man drinking soju. Drunk young men walked by.

Jihyun

Every day at lunch Jihyun would help Justin with his ramyeon. Justin always got Jajangmyun ramyeon. Justin had never eaten ramyeon in his whole life until he went to Korea. There he was—eating ramyeon at a lunch table with four Korean women holding metal chopsticks.

Justin could never tell when his ramyeon was done. He had to ask Jihyun. She would look at his ramyeon and say, "No, more."

Justin would say, "I'm so hungry."

After a few minutes, Jihyun would tell him it was time, Justin would go to the bathroom and dump out the water, go back to the lunch table, pour in the brown seasoning packet, and eat his ramyeon. Jihyun always ate a packed lunch. She ate a lot of dried sardines. To Justin the sardines looked old and sad. Jihyun would eat rice with an over-easy egg cooked in the morning, Jihyun was very helpful to Justin. She was his neighbor. She had taken him to the library once to show him where it was. She showed him where the best restaurants were in the area. They once ate chicken together at work.

Hiyun was super nice. She seemed to have no sense of self. Whatever the boss Mr. Park wanted, she did without question. Whatever her parents wanted, she did without question. She was twenty-eight and still followed her curfew perfectly. She always held the door open for Justin.

Justin would daydream about Jihyun, about her tall skinny body. She was five foot seven, with a cute body, her skin pale white, which Justin didn't like but he thought if she returned to America with him then he could convince her to get a tan. Justin knew she was a virgin. He wondered how her vagina felt. He wondered what it would be like to be a twenty-eight-year-old virgin.

Justin saw them living in Ohio. They owned a house, working on a thirty-year mortgage. Justin would have a good job. He didn't specify in his imagination what the job was, but he had one. Justin would get Jihyun a job at the Red Lobster where he used to work. There was a Korean woman already working there. They could be friends, they could talk about kimchee or something, drink soju, eat ramyeon together. Yeah, that sounded great.

Jihyun would cook Justin food every day. Justin would teach her to cook cheeseburgers and spaghetti. She would do it happily, probably even feel sincere about the cooking of American food. She would clean the house. Nothing would be filthy. Everything would be nice and clean.

Jihyun would get pregnant with his babies. These babies would be mixed and awesome-looking. Justin would marry a foreign woman, which would make him cool in some circles. Justin would bring Jihyun to his parents' house. Jihyun would love his parents, because she was Korean and liked things involving family. Everything would be great. Maddie was too American. She liked her independence too much. He needed an old-fashioned woman. Marrying Jihyun would be like traveling back in time, like he was getting into a time machine and marrying a woman from the 50s. He could become his father. He could become normal.

He wouldn't be able to have intellectual conversations about anything, but maybe his sister was right. Love wasn't about intellectual conversations but about protection and sharing. Then it would occur to him that a twenty-eight-year-old virgin was pretty weird, that she might be suffering from a severe mental problem, that sex with her might be really awkward, that she must have extreme intimacy issues if she had never even had a one night stand, that she wouldn't even have taken the chance to do it once, she must have felt inadequate or something. It explained the Japanese racism thing he thought, explained the whole teaching of little kids, feeling inferior and scared of adults, especially adult men. Justin wondered what her dad did to cause such a fear. He had assumptions, but the data was inconclusive. Eventually he would stop thinking about Jihyun and think about what he was going to eat for dinner.

Sometimes Jihyun would daydream about marrying Justin and going to America, but the only outlets of information she had concerning America were *Gossip Girl* and *Sex and the City*. She had no idea what kind of life Justin lived in America. It had never occurred to her to ask him about his personal life there. She was not allowed to ask her father questions. The idea of having a personal emotional relationship with a male did not even occur to her. She imagined living in New York City with Justin. She didn't work. She spent her days taking care of the house. Justin would work and provide her with money to go shopping. She would wear fantastic outfits like the characters in *Gossip Girl* and *Sex and the City*. She would have such nice outfits. She would be like those Gangnam girls who had the best clothes. She wouldn't have to shop in the Sineung Underground Mall anymore. She hated those clothes. She wanted to go to Gangnam and shop.

She thought about how clean she would keep the apartment, how she would cook meals for Justin, and he would be so happy. She would pack him a lunch for work and he would be excited every day at lunch to see what she made him. She felt enthusiastic about cooking lunches and packing them. Sometimes she would think about sex with Justin. She had never had sex though: the images her mind created all came from Japanese movies that played on cable at night. She had seen a Japanese movie where the woman had no shirt on, and the man was tightly holding her. She assumed that was sex. She didn't want to have Japanese sex though, because she hated the Japanese. She hoped it would be American sex. But she had no idea how Americans had sex. Sometimes she had sexual thoughts about Nate Archibald from *Gossip Girl*. She didn't think Justin was as good-looking as Nate Archibald, but he was handsome. He had blue eyes. He was good enough.

But Justin had a girlfriend, an American girlfriend. American girls were sluts. They had sex. Jihyun knew she couldn't compete with that. It made her hate American women a little. When everyone went out to dinner, all the teachers, Justin and Maddie, Jihyun never directly asked Maddie a question or brought attention to herself. Her theory on social interaction with an adult was, be quiet, be polite, until it is over.

The electronic bell rung and lunch was over.

Morning in Korea

The smartphone alarm went off at 6:30AM. It was a soft song. It was an app she'd downloaded, a special app that played soft songs every fifteen minutes, until eventually she woke up. The songs sounded like electronic crickets and mosquitoes playing synthesizers while on Vicodin.

Maddie had to wake up early. She worked at a kinder hagwon. (A kinder hagwon is where wealthy people send their children to learn every subject in English starting at the age of four. Justin, her boyfriend, worked at a cram hagwon, where normal-income people send their kids to learn English for an hour after school starting at the age of nine, while the poor sent their children nowhere—the poor did not learn English, the poor did not pass the examinations to get into college, and they would end up working construction or at Kimbap shops, McDonald's like in America, drink Soju, eat Ramyeon, die one day.)

Maddie sat up in bed. She didn't want to get out of bed. She walked over to the neon green French press she bought at Starbucks. She heated water and started the coffee. She needed coffee or she would feel very bad throughout the whole day.

Maddie showered. She didn't wash her hair. Her hair was too curly and thick. She was half-Slovenian and Italian, but in Korea she was just American and white, washing it would make it too frizzy. She liked her hair because it made her unique but at the same time it was a hassle. Maddie kept her hair dry. She was alone in the apartment. She washed her armpits and her face.

The apartment was empty. There was no sound. Her boyfriend was in Seongnam. She was in Gunpo. Her friends were in America. She felt alone. Alone was a feeling, oppressing, it crept up in her muscles, it made her stomach hurt. Sometimes it gave her a headache. Feeling alone and knowing she was alone conquered her at times and she did not want to clean her apartment. She went over to her MAC and put on 8-tracks. She turned on a witch house soundtrack, turned it up loud. She needed her music. The sun came up. She stood naked before her window. She looked out her window. There was a mountain between the buildings she could see. She liked looking at the mountain tucked between the buildings. In the summer she hiked Mount Bukhansan. She hiked up to the Buddhist temples. She walked inside the temples. They were small with tigers painted on the walls. On the back of one of the temples was a painting of a boy carrying a rope chasing butterflies. She didn't know what it meant, what the story was. Was it impossible to catch butterflies with a rope? Maddie never thought about butterflies—she hardly ever considered bugs. At the temple she lit incense for the Buddha. She was Catholic but since everyone was doing it, she did it also. She gave a donation and drank tea. From the temples she could see Seoul, the center of it, where all the power resonated. The buildings flowed like a river among the mountains, white spikes sprouting out of the ground. Maddie knew the Han River was down there settled in among the white spikes and mountains, but she could not see the river. Maddie wondered if before 1900, before the buildup in Seoul, if a person could see the river down there from Mount Bukhansan, but there was no one to ask. They were all dead or they couldn't speak English. She loved to look at temples. She looked at the fantastic painted tigers on the walls of the temples. She loved them, she liked cats, but she was more of a lion fan because she was a Leo. One time Justin played a video of tigers and lions fighting and she said she could not watch it because she didn't want to watch lions get hurt by those stupid tigers.

Maddie sat before a small mirror, a tiny little mirror. She straightened her hair. She decided her hair was too wild that day to show the kids. They might laugh at her. She had to get her makeup right. The women of Korea were all perfect and beautiful. There were so many pretty girls in Seoul who woke up early to make sure their makeup was perfect, she had to compete with all the Korean girls. She had to compete with all the girls. She felt terrible inside, lonely, missing her friends. If she could put the right makeup on, if she could make herself beautiful, then no one would know how she felt inside, no one would know she felt anxiety, that she was sleepy, that she wanted just to go back home and sleep. She put on her makeup, first the eyes, then the cheeks, then the lips. After an hour she finished. Of course she went over the time allotted to do her makeup. She was running behind.

She swore to herself, shit fuck damn goddamn morning job, she put on her coat, grabbed her purse and went out the door. Maddie always said she went to Korea to test herself. She had to prove something to herself. Maddie believed in personal tests. She had that Nietzsche spirit, that Übermensch spirit. She believed that people should test themselves. She believed that she was above the concerns of other people. When asked

about politics she merely responded, "You speakin' games."
She considered sex 'something to be done when very drunk.'
She considered popular culture 'something to be analyzed to
find out how the masses are ruining their lives.' She did not
concern herself with the ambitions of humankind. She had
her own dreams. Her test though didn't lead her to working
in the Congo or Saudi Arabia because she knew those places
were too dangerous for a woman. Korea was safe in terms of
violence. Korea had running water, electricity, and a legitimate
subway system. She took the best test she could find.

Maddie was the first on her dad's side of the family to graduate
college. She was the first to travel to Asia. She was the first in
many things and proud of it. She considered herself a hero to
her family.

She left her ten-story building and walked outside. It was chilly.
Koreans walked the streets endlessly. She had gone outside
several times at five in the morning and Koreans were still
walking the streets. The sidewalks were never empty. Maddie
was from a small town in Ohio, a town of 1,500. So small,
she thought. It was an Amish town. Carriages carrying Amish
would always be on the streets. She grew up in a world with
horses and farms. There was even a horse stall at Walmart. The
center of life in her town was Walmart. She didn't like any of
it. She wanted out of it. No one ever walked the streets in her
small town. Sometimes the Amish children would ride funny
scooters down the street.

Maddie looked at all the signs and buildings. She felt happy
being a person who takes the subway. She felt happy she had
made it to Korea. She felt happy she had found a place to
live on the other side of the planet. She walked through the
Sanbon subway area. The buildings shot up fifteen stories.

The signs went up to the tops of the buildings. She liked looking at Korean signs. She liked trying to read the Hangul. She could read and pronounce Hangul, but she didn't know many words so most signs were lost on her, but she had been there for seven months and had learned some words. Sometimes she would spot a word she knew and feel happy. The sky was blue and everything was pretty and good. She walked up the ramp to the subway. She reached into her pocket and found no subway card, then she reached into her purse and found no money to get a taxi. She panicked but then realized she could use her bankcard to get a new T-money card. Hope was not lost. A sudden feeling of relief went through her body. Then she opened her wallet and found no bank card. She felt then in her body that she was fucked. Panic. She would be late for work.

Maddie turned around and started to run.

Running running running.

Terrible feelings rose up in her. This was the test, she thought. Maddie played sports in school. She knew how to run, she was not a weak person. Running running running. She really hated her life at that moment. She hated Korea while she was running. Maddie didn't look at the pretty signs covered with Hangul when she was running. She didn't try to listen for the magpies singing. She felt nothing but anxiety, an extreme over-coming sense of foreboding and fear. She didn't want to be late to work, she didn't want her boss to know she was late, she didn't want her co-teachers to think she was lazy and stupid and that she couldn't remember her T-money card and bank card like a normal person, running running running.

She felt horrible running. No one in Seoul jogged and she wasn't dressed as a jogger. She was dressed as a pretty girl about to go to work. She kept thinking about what the Koreans must be thinking about her, then it occurred to her that some of her co-teachers must be going to work at the same time, that one of them could see her. She was terrified of that happening. Of course they would ask why she was running. She would have to explain. One fear led to another fear. This was all part of the test, she told herself. It was true, it was a test.

She made it back to her apartment. She grabbed her subway card and bank card, grabbed cash from the coffee table. She grabbed 10,000 won. The terrible feelings started to subside but the day had been ruined. The whole day would be nothing but a shadow of the morning's hell.

Maddie went outside and found a taxi to drive her to work. She scolded herself. Instead of spending 1,200 won on a subway ride, she ended up spending 4,300 won on a taxi.

Taking the Bus
from Anyang

The morning was chilly. There were two inches of snow on the ground. Justin walked outside at nine in the morning. He could see his breath. He bought a warm can of coffee. It was a quiet early December morning. It was Christmastime in America. Everyone in America was getting ready for the holidays. They were buying presents, Bing Crosby was playing on the radio, lights were being put on trees. Everyone was getting excited for Christmas. The only place in Korea that wanted to celebrate Christmas was Caffe Bene. They put up cute decorations and played random covers of Christmas songs that Justin had never heard play in America. No one else in Korea cared about Christmas. Justin kept trying to remember Christmases that came before. He would recollect the Christmas of 1989 in his grandmother's house, everyone sitting around in a circle handing out presents, Christmas of 1991 when Uncle Henry's pond froze over and everyone got to go ice skating on Christmas night. Justin's theory was that if he could remember Christmas hard enough, he would not need America to have a great Christmas.

The bus stop was in front of Maddie's high-rise. He stood out there waiting for the bus. There was a computer screen thing that notified everyone when the buses would come. It said four minutes for bus 3500 and after four minutes it would say jam-she-hu. Justin didn't know what jam-she-hu meant exactly. He assumed it meant "Bus get here."

Justin had irritable bowel syndrome. He felt horrible about taking long bus and subway rides. At least when he drove a car in America he would be able to stop and go to a Subway to shit. Subways always had bathrooms and the employees never cared about asking you to order. There were no Subways in Korea. Justin never knew where the bathrooms were and he hated it. Justin felt a little rumble in his stomach. Things were shifting around. He knew it was bad but the bus was coming soon.

He stood there, in anxiety. Should he go back up to Maddie's apartment and shit or get on the bus and hope it went away. Justin decided to get on the bus. It was packed full of people. Justin jammed himself in. The bus was so crowded that a man's hand was on his leg and the back of his hand was on a woman's ass. Justin's stomach started to feel okay. He felt he could make it.

He stood there, smashed in, unable to move or even look around or even look down. He was forced to look at the back of a young woman's hair. The bus stopped in the middle of the highway.

Justin got off the bus. He knew he had to shit. He had to wait at a small open-air bus stop in the middle of nowhere. There were no buildings, nothing, just mountains and forest. On the other side of the highway was a bus stop with a gas station with a bathroom, but trying to cross a twelve lane highway seemed impossible.

The sky was a beautiful blue. A few small white clouds floated high up, just passing slowly in and out of view. It was a wonderful morning. Why did he need to shit so bad? He looked at the computer screen for bus 333. The computer said it would be twenty minutes, then another twenty minutes home. He didn't have forty minutes. Maybe fifteen but not forty. The clock was ticking.

Justin remembered shitting himself in America. He had shit himself in the morning driving to class. He was driving to school and couldn't make it. Three minutes before he got to a parking space, boom, his ass exploded into his pants. It was wet and sad. He started crying. He was a thirty-year-old man in his car, crying with shit in his pants.

The other time was horrible. He was with his sister. They were coming home from Chili's at night. He began sweating. He kept telling his sister to drive faster. Four minutes before he could have made it to a toilet, at a red light, he got out of the car and ran behind some trees, pushed his pants down, then shit, but he had never squat-shit in his life and got shit on the back of his pants. It was horrible. He began crying. He felt defeated by life whenever he shit himself.

Justin knew it was completely possible that he might shit himself. He had done it before, therefore logic implied it could happen again. Justin looked up at the mountains surrounding the bus stop. He knew he had napkins in his bookbag because he recently had a cold and had to blow his nose a lot. He knew he could squat-shit because his hagwon had a squat toilet and he had become very good at squat-shitting. Justin thought it was a pretty morning. It would be a good nature shit, a shit with the trees, a shit among the bugs and dead leaves.

Justin started walking away from the bus stop. The people at the bus stop knew where he was going. They looked and laughed in their heads. He walked to where the fence ended. He saw a little path. He figured this was the Shit Path. He walked up the path. The mountain was not steep, a slight incline. He had walked in the forest many times in Ohio, Pennsylvania, the Rockies, and Yellowstone. He knew how to walk in a forest, over steep inclines, but he had to do all this walking while having to shit badly.

He didn't know how far up he should go. No matter how far he walked up the mountain he could still see the highway, but he realized that drivers would be focusing on the road, and the only person who might notice he was shitting would be a passenger bored out of their mind, and they would just laugh and maybe tell the driver, and that would be the end of the conversation. No one would call the police. They would probably just assume that he was some sad incontinent ajeossi and not a foreigner with irritable bowel syndrome.

Justin found the perfect place, a nice piece of level ground with a tree to hide behind. He pushed his pants down, squatted, put his right hand on the tree behind him and shit. He laughed while he did it. He thought about how funny he must look. He wondered if God was watching, if God would take some of his sins away for shitting next to a highway, if he was erasing any bad karma. He wiped his ass, then walked back down the mountain.

He had no way of washing his hands. He was deeply afraid of giving himself pink eye. He smelled his hands. They smelled okay. He emerged from the mountain onto the highway. The people at the bus stop didn't look at him. They probably assumed he just went up there to piss. Probably all of them had pissed on that mountain, Justin told himself. Bus 333 came and Justin got on it.

Infinite vs. Teen Top

Jihae walked down an alley, a thirteen-year-old girl, her hair black, long down past her shoulders, bangs going down to her eyes, almost hiding them. She wore a school uniform, a simple dress and white shirt with her name on it. Every weekday she would leave school and go home. No one would be home. She had no brothers or sisters, no cat or dog. She went to the cupboard and took out a bag of ramyeon, made the ramyeon and sat at the kitchen table eating it. Her mother told her never to eat food in the living room. The living room was five feet away. The kitchen and living room were the same room.

After she finished her ramyeon, she did her math homework. She went through each problem, then checked them over. She knew when her dad got home from work at 9PM he would ask to see her math homework. He was an engineer. He knew his math. Jihae was proud of her father, who was so good at math. He would check every answer and see if they were correct. If she got every answer right, he would give Jihae a candy bar. Jihae wanted to make her father proud that she was like him, so good at math.

Jihae's mother was at work. Jihae's mother would never help her with homework, but would yell at her that she needed to do it. Jihae loved her mom but didn't like spending time with her alone. Her mother would often come home with a bottle of makkoli. She would put her purse down, talk about work for ten minutes, swirl her bottle of makkoli, pour herself a glass, and watch television.

Her parents never made food at home on the weekdays. They got home from work too late. Her father would order either Chinese food or Korean food from local places. A delivery man on a scooter would bring the food. Jihae liked to eat Jajangmyun from the Chinese place and Kimchee Bokkeumbap from the Korean place. Sometimes she would get Jappong from the Chinese place. Her family would eat at the table while watching television.

Jihae's mother drank makkoli almost every night. She said she couldn't sleep without it. Most nights her father would not drink. Her parents did not talk a lot, just small talk. Sometimes, about once a month, her father would go out with his friends. They would go out all night. Her mother would pace the floor. She looked worried and sad. Jihae would ask her mother what was wrong. Her mother would tell her to shut up and go to sleep. Jihae would go to her small bedroom. She would lie in her bed and listen to Infinite on her headphones. Jihea couldn't sleep those nights. She knew what was coming.

Around 11PM, her mother would begin text messaging frantically. Eventually her father would step in the door. He would be drunk. He would smell of soju and beer. Her mother would start screaming. He would sit in a chair and look down. Jihae would turn her headphones up as loud as they could go, but the screaming was too loud. After ten minutes of screaming, her father would pick something up and smash it. When Jihae was five, she ran out to the living room to see what the crashing was. Her mother slapped her in the face. She ran back to her room and never ran out again.

She would hear the smashing of objects, and screaming. It was endless. She didn't like it. She would blame her father for ruining her night. Couldn't he just stay home. Couldn't he just sit and drink makkoli with her mother. Sometimes she would hear the word '창녀' but she didn't understand what it meant. She had never heard that word on television. She knew some swear words, but she had never heard that word.

After half an hour, her parents would settle down and go to sleep. She would have at least a month of peace before it happened again.

Jihae finished her ramyeon, changed from her school uniform to her hagwon clothes. Jihae didn't have a lot of clothes. Her parents both had jobs but her parents spent all their money on things like the nice apartment and the car they owned. Jihae never understood why they needed a car. She barely ever rode in it, and neither did her mother. Only her father drove the car. She didn't understand why her father needed a car when Seongnam had such good public transportation. Every day she would change into a white shirt and short black shorts. She would always tuck in her white t-shirt. She would look at herself in the mirror and make sure she looked good, that she didn't have any food on her face, and then she would brush her teeth.

Jihae texted Eunmi to meet her before hagwon at the local dukbokki shop. Eunmi didn't go home after school. She was slightly overweight and her face was round and her hair was black and long. She was thirteen years old. Eunmi didn't want to go home. She lived with her grandparents. Her parents were two sad soju drunks. She hardly ever saw them. She didn't know what jobs they had. She didn't know where they lived. Her mother's parents took her in. Her grandparents owned a vegetable shop. They would go to the vegetable shop at nine in the morning and her grandparents would not come home until ten at night sometimes. One of them might come home early and leave the other one there, but they were too tired to talk to her or spend time with her. Eunmi would arrive at the hagwon at 4:30 even though she didn't have class until 6:30. After her class ended at 7:30 she would go home and eat mandoo or ramyeon alone watching television. She was excited to be alone because she could pick the shows she wanted. When her grandparents were home she had to watch whatever show they wanted. On those nights she would go into her room, do homework, and listen to her headphones.

Eunmi met Jihae at the dukbokki shop. They bowed and laughed when they saw each other. They sat down at a small table and ordered dukbokki. They talked about delicious dukbokki. Every day they would start the same fight. Who was better: Infinite or Teen Top. Jihae thought Infinite was better. Eunmi thought Teen Top was better.

"Oh no, Teen Top is better, Ricky is so cute," said Eunmi.

"No, you are stupid, Infinite is better. Woohyun is cute. Woohyun is so cute," said Jihae.

"You are crazy, Ricky is cuter than Woohyun."

Jihae took out a notebook. It was her Infinite notebook. She wrote down all the lyrics to their songs. On most pages she just wrote "Woohyun" over and over and over again.

우현 우현 우현 우현 우현 우현 우현 우현 우현 우현
우현 우현 우현 우현 우현 우현 우현 우현 우현 우현
우현 우현 우현 우현 우현 우현 우현 우현 우현 우현
우현 우현 우현 우현 우현 우현 우현 우현 우현 우현
우현 우현 우 현 우현 우현 우현 우현 우현 우현 우현
우현 우현 우현 우현 우현 우현 우현 우현 우현 우현
우현 우현 우현 우현 우현 우현 우현 우현 우현 우현
우현 우현 우현 우현 우현 우현 우현 우현 우현 우현
우현 우현 우현 우현 우현 우현 우현 우현 우현 우현
우현 우현 우 현 우현 우현 우현 우현 우현 우현 우현
우현 우현 우현 우현 우현 우현 우현 우현 우현 우현
우현 우현 우현 우현 우현 우현 우현 우현 우현 우현
우현 우현 우현 우현 우현 우현 우현 우현 우현 우현
우현 우현 우현 우현 우현 우현 우현 우현 우현 우현
우현 우현 우 현 우현 우현 우현 우현 우현 우현 우현
우현 우현 우현 우현 우현 우현 우현 우현 우현 우현
우현 우현 우현 우현 우현 우현 우현 우현 우현 우현
우현 우현 우현 우현 우현 우현 우현 우현 우현 우현

Writing 우현 gave Jihae a feeling of peace. She would write
우현 very neatly, like she was doing calligraphy. She told
Eunmi she was worried about Woohyun because he had to go
to the military soon. She expressed tenderly that she would
miss him, and hoped he went back to singing when he got out
of the military. Even though Eunmi did not like Infinite, she
felt sad when KPOP stars had to go to the military.

Eunmi took out her notebook, but she wasn't as obsessed with
KPOP as Jihae was. She was obsessed with English. Eunmi
wasn't pretty. No one ever told her she was pretty. She wasn't
the smartest either. She was always in the top ten but she was
never the smartest. She would practice her English for hours
every day. She would write out English words over and over

again, making sure she spelled every word correctly. She had a three day system. She would learn a new word on the first day, then for three days she wrote the new word twenty times a day for three days. When she did that they always stuck in her head. Justin Teacher showed her how to find TV shows in English online. She began watching English television dramas like *Gossip Girls* and *True Blood*. It was hard to find those shows with Hangul subtitles but after a while of searching she would be able to do it. She wanted to be the best in English. She wanted to prove to the world she was good at something. Writing English words and watching English television took her to a far-away place, where her parents and grandparents and Korea could not find her. She felt like an astronaut of English, traveling to distant verbs, prepositions, articles, planets of adjectives and adverbs. She loved it. She was determined to one day become an English teacher, to live in an English-speaking country and forget everything that came before. A few times she asked Justin Teacher to take her back to America. He would always laugh, but she was serious.

After they finished their dukbokki, they went to the English hagwon. They went in the computer room, which was also the foreign teacher's office. The foreign teacher, Justin, was sitting at his desk looking up things on Wikipedia. Jihae and Eunmi went over to him.

"Justin Teacher, how are you?" said Eunmi.

"I'm fine, how are you?" said Justin Teacher.

Jihae said, "Who do you like better, Infinite or Teen Top?"

Justin Teacher said, "I like Miss A."

"No, Justin Teacher, but which one? Infinite or Teen Top?"

Justin Teacher sat in his chair. He felt confused by the question. He tried to remember hearing either of their songs. He decided he liked Infinite better and he said, "I like Infinite."

Eunmi screamed, "Oh no, Justin Teacher!"

Jihae and Eunmi went to the computers to do their computer homework. They put on headphones and listened to words in English and then had to type them out. There was also a game they could play where they had to shoot bunny rabbits with English words on their backs (the headphones said an English word and they had to then shoot the bunny with the correct word on its back).

The computer room was full of students, some as young as nine years old, some as old as fourteen. The boys would gather together and play games on their cellphones, the girls would group together in another place and talk about KPOP boy bands. The girls and boys hardly ever spoke to each other. Jihae and Eunmi would spend hours walking around the hagwon talking to people. They would get excited every time a friend came in. They would talk and laugh, then their friend would go to class, then a new group of friends would come in, and they would talk to them. Every day it went like that, two young girls spending their hours hanging out in an English hagwon.

The Tiger
Painter

Jungsu sat in his art studio. He ate a stick of kimbap. He stared at his latest painting. It was a tiger.

Jungsu only painted tigers.

He never painted people. He couldn't do it. He didn't feel that people were worth painting. Sometimes he painted trees. He liked to walk the local mountains in the fall. He would go off the paths carrying a digital camera. He would look for the perfect tree. He believed there were perfect trees. He had read three books about the trees of Korea. He considered himself a Korean tree expert. A person could point at any tree in Korea and Jungsu would be able to name what type of tree it was. He wasn't a botanist, he was an artist, a painter. He had gone to Hongik University and majored in art. Junsu's parents were wealthy. They owned over thirty high-rise apartment buildings. They made money for Jungsu to travel the world. He had been to England, Italy, France, and Germany—basically all of Europe—and he had been to America and Canada and spent a night in Tijuana, and he had been to China, Japan, Cambodia, and Vietnam. He had seen the world and always went to the museums when visiting a country. He looked at their trees. He liked trees and tigers.

Jungsu was twenty-eight years old and had never held a real job. He made money producing tiger, tree, and bird paintings for calendars and Korean magazines. For a while he drew covers for novels, but they always wanted him to paint humans, which he didn't like. At night Junsu would go out to Hongdae and drink. Almost every night he would sit in the Motto Bar or Susie Q's and listen to western music and drink himself into a stupor. His parents never asked him what he was doing. Sometimes they would tell him to get married, but they knew he would never listen. Jungsu had a brother and sister. They had both gotten married and had good professional jobs. His parents thought, 'Well, two out of three isn't bad, and why not have an artist in the family?' He gave the family color, and a sense of refinement, and they had enough money to support him anyway, so why not spend the money on their son? (While they spent their money on their son to do almost nothing but have a good time, they had a mass of minimum wage employees who could barely afford to eat.)

Jungsu traveled Korea looking at paintings of tigers. Tiger paintings were often found in Buddhist temples. Jungsu was not Buddhist but he didn't care. He wanted to see the tiger paintings. He would travel all the way to Gyeongnam Province to visit a tiger painting he saw in a book. He would always get really close to the painting and just stare with a calm expression. When he was at the MoMa, he stood there for two hours staring at van Gogh paintings. He wanted to understand every brush stroke. He wanted to understand. Twice a month he would go to the Samsung Art Museum and stare at the Rothkos. He would get really close to the Rothkos. He knew that painting was a series of brush strokes. Each brush stroke made the painting. Brush strokes were like trees in a forest. Each tree mattered, each living leaf mattered, each dead leaf mattered because the dead leaves became the soil that nourished future trees. Each plant mattered and all the bugs mattered. He always enjoyed finding a bug. When a bug died in a forest it too became nutrition for the trees. Societies were full of people. Each person made that society, each single brush stroke made the painting, each word became a book. Junsu worried endlessly about his brush strokes. He never thought his brush strokes were right.

He couldn't sleep at night unless he drank. He never knew if he was being honest. He wanted to be honest like western artists. He told himself that the one thing you couldn't buy was the talent to make an honest piece of art. His parents could never buy that for him. If he became a lawyer or business owner, his parents could his buy education and buy his business, but his parents could not buy honesty.

Three years earlier he made a great painting of a tiger. Everyone liked it. It was put into a calendar for the month of March. It was put on magnets and even some holiday cards. The painting was later put up in a gallery in Hongdae. It was his best piece. He didn't know how he did it. He was bored on a Saturday and was sitting at his parents' house eating dinner. His mother kept asking him when he was going to get married. He had finished his military duty and he had finished college and it was time to get married and have some kids, get a job, start his life. After the annoying conversation with his mother, Jungsu got a taxi and rode to his studio and painted his famous tiger. Jungsu didn't even remember the conversation he'd had with his parents. He only remembered painting it.

Jungsu ate his kimbap. He wanted to paint a tiger, a real one, a tiger that would symbolize how he felt, but he didn't know how to be honest like he was that day. He kept painting tigers similar to the one he painted that day, replicating the same tiger, over and over. Jungsu started to wonder if he only had one true tiger in him.

Jungsu finished his kimbap and walked to the Motto Bar. He sat with his girlfriend, Soonjoo. Soonjoo was pretty and had wealthy parents as well. Her parents owned a chain of bars popular in Seoul. She had finished college and was spending her nights tending bar at one of her parents' clubs. She smoked a pack of Parliament Lights a day and never went five minutes without texting on KakaoTalk, a Korean texting app. Sometimes she felt extreme anxiety over which emoticon to use.

Jungsu said to Soonjoo, "I can't paint anymore."

"Well, stop painting those stupid tigers," she said while typing on KakaoTalk on her phone.

Jungsu just sat there. He didn't understand. Why wouldn't someone want to paint tigers? Tigers were wonderful.

He said, "I need to go to the bathroom."

Jungsu walked up the stairs and out the door. He kept walking. He was alone. He didn't like being alone. He wanted friends, but something was wrong with him. Ever since he was little, he was bothered by the trees and tigers. They seemed so much more beautiful than people. Trees were taller and lived longer and gave birth to oxygen. Tigers were bigger, stronger, faster, and could kill anything except maybe elephants. He had never heard of a tiger killing an elephant. He started to wonder about anacondas. If he lived in South America he would paint anacondas. If he was in America he would paint black bears. If he was in Africa he would paint lions. While he was walking, Soonjoo texted him: "You only paint tigers to feel normal, and because you know pictures of tigers are popular in Korea. Why don't you paint something more complex, that doesn't get you immediate validation."

He texted back: "I paint tigers because they are beautiful."

He walked through the streets. No one and nothing looked at him. The people walking past him didn't care he existed and neither did the neon lights of the buildings. People walked around with their tiny dogs and the dogs did not even bark at him.

He walked to the Mapo Bridge that crossed over the Han River. He stood there cold. Jungsu wanted to be original, he wanted to have magic brush strokes, brush strokes as strong as Rothko's, but instead he didn't get anywhere. He wanted to paint an image that would live on a Buddhist temple for a thousand years. He wanted and wanted and wanted. Instead of wanting objects and titles like his brother and sister, he wanted the perfect tiger. Now he wanted to die. He got everything he ever wanted in life. He asked his parents and they gave, and now he wanted to die, he wanted death, he was alone in a world where being alone was not allowed, he was weak in a world that demanded strength. A horrible sound was crushing him, like white noise static blaring feedback corroding every good thought he could ever have. He couldn't remember his last good thought, his last good day. He asked himself as he walked to the center of the bridge if he even enjoyed looking at trees and tigers, if he only did so to create more paintings, if he even enjoyed painting or only did it because he needed validation for doing something, for doing anything. He couldn't play piano because he was tone-deaf, he wasn't good at math, he wasn't good at English as he always forgot the 'A' and confused 'to' and 'of.' But he could always draw. He started drawing cartoons, then moved on to replicating pictures he had taken, but he was never that good. His friend Jiyong from college went on to become an artist recognized by all of Korea. He kept thinking about Jiyong. Jiyong painted weird squares and triangles. Sometimes he just took shoelaces and wrapped them around things. Everyone loved Jiyong. When Jiyong and Jungsu were at Hongik University, everyone thought they were the two most talented painters at the school. They both won the same awards, they both sat all night talking about the same things, but Jiyong told Jungsu constantly, "You have to move on, try new things."

Three weeks earlier, Jiyong made a KakaoTalk art installation piece where a mannequin of a Korean girl was trapped inside KakaoTalk by chains and she couldn't get free. The art installation was featured in many magazines and Jiyong sold it to a museum in New York City for over 100,000 dollars. Jungsu had never made over 10,000 won in one year, let alone any American dollars. Jungsu felt he had to kill himself. He realized that his mind could never escape his obsession with trees and tigers. His mind wasn't capable of creating a piece of art that the art world liked. Tigers were from a bygone age where Buddhist temples were still being painted, and all the Buddhist temples were already painted. Nobody was building any new Buddhist temples. He wasn't even a Buddhist.

Jungsu kept thinking about Jiyong. He didn't blame Jiyong for what he had done. He didn't know if it was sociological or genetic but he just didn't have the talent Jiyong had. He felt that he had talent, he could paint trees and tigers, but he had a talent for something no one wanted anymore. He looked at the river and jumped.

They found his body floating the next day.

When Jiyong heard the news of his friend, he constructed a giant bridge and then made thirty tigers jumping off the bridge, some standing close to the rail, some suspended in midair, some floating in the water below. The art installation was giant and took up the whole bottom floor of the Samsung Art Museum. When Jiyong was interviewed concerning his new creation, he talked of his friend's death and how much pain it caused. Magazines in Europe and America began interviewing Jiyong about Korea's suicide problem.